THE LEGEND OF THE WINDIGO

❋ A TALE FROM ❋
NATIVE NORTH AMERICA

RETOLD BY GAYLE ROSS
PAINTINGS BY MURV JACOB

DIAL BOOKS FOR YOUNG READERS
NEW YORK

copol

Published by Dial Books for Young Readers
A Division of Penguin Books USA Inc.
375 Hudson Street
New York, New York 10014

Designed by Julie Rauer
Printed in Hong Kong
First Edition
1 3 5 7 9 10 8 6 4 2

Library of Congress Cataloging in Publication Data
Ross, Gayle.
The legend of the Windigo: a tale from native North America/
retold by Gayle Ross; paintings by Murv Jacob.—1st ed.
p. cm.
ISBN 0-8037-1897-7.—ISBN 0-8037-1898-5 (lib. bdg.)
1. Windigos. 2. Algonquian Indians—Folklore. I. Jacob, Murv. II. Title.
E99.A35R67 1996 398.24'54—dc20 95-6333 CIP AC

The artwork was rendered in acrylics
on watercolor paper.

To my adopted brother,
Ron Evans, with love —G.R.

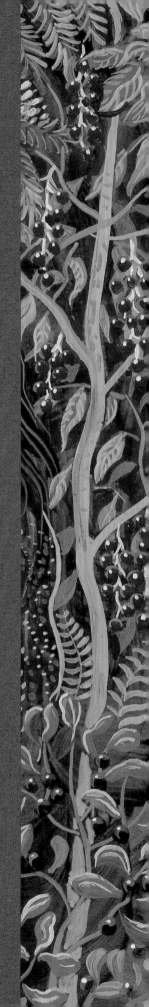

LONG AGO, DEEP IN THE FORESTS OF THE NORTH WOODLANDS, there lived a village of people. These people followed the ways of their ancestors: hunting deer, trapping beaver, and fishing in the

bright blue lakes that lay scattered like jewels across the land.
But one day trouble came to that ancient village.

It began when a young warrior went out hunting overnight and did not return in the morning. A few days later a young woman was missing from the village. Now, that young man had courted that young woman, but her father had not wanted them to marry. And so the people said, "Perhaps they have run away together." And they thought no more about it. But as the days passed and the couple did not return, a sense of fear began to spread through the village. Fear changed to panic when another person vanished, and another.

Then the people knew that a Windigo had come to live in their woods. Now, a Windigo is a giant creature made of stone with eyes like deep caves that hypnotize human beings. When a human looks into the eyes of a Windigo, he is in the Windigo's power and is helpless to escape. In his true form the Windigo is taller than the tallest tree in the forest, but he can change his shape at will. Whatever shape he takes, two things never change, and those are the bottomless black pools of his eyes. The Windigo is a cannibal. He feeds on the people.

Because a Windigo is made of stone, he cannot be harmed by an arrow or a lance. From the beginning of time the human beings had fled in terror before the Windigo. If a Windigo came to live in a forest where people were, the people moved away—far, far away.

But these people loved the land they lived in and did not want to move. They came together in a great council to talk over what they must do.

Some people were frightened and said, "We must leave this place or the Windigo will take us all." Others said, "We do not want to leave our homes. Our ancestors sleep in this land."

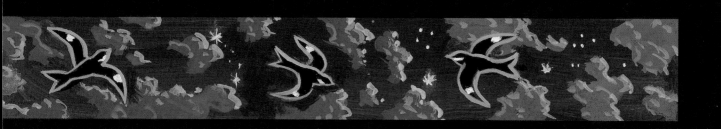

Finally it was decided that the elders, the wise ones, would seek the help and guidance of the spirit protectors of their land. Through prayer, fasting, and ceremony the elders would surely be shown the right thing to do. "We must build the sacred sweat lodge today," the people declared, "and tonight the elders will purify themselves and pray for help."

Young, straight willow trees were gathered for the frame of the sweat lodge, and women brought buffalo hides to cover it. The sacred fire was lit and tended all afternoon as it burned down to a deep bed of white-hot coals, heating the stones buried in the heart of the fire. Finally, when darkness fell, all was ready.

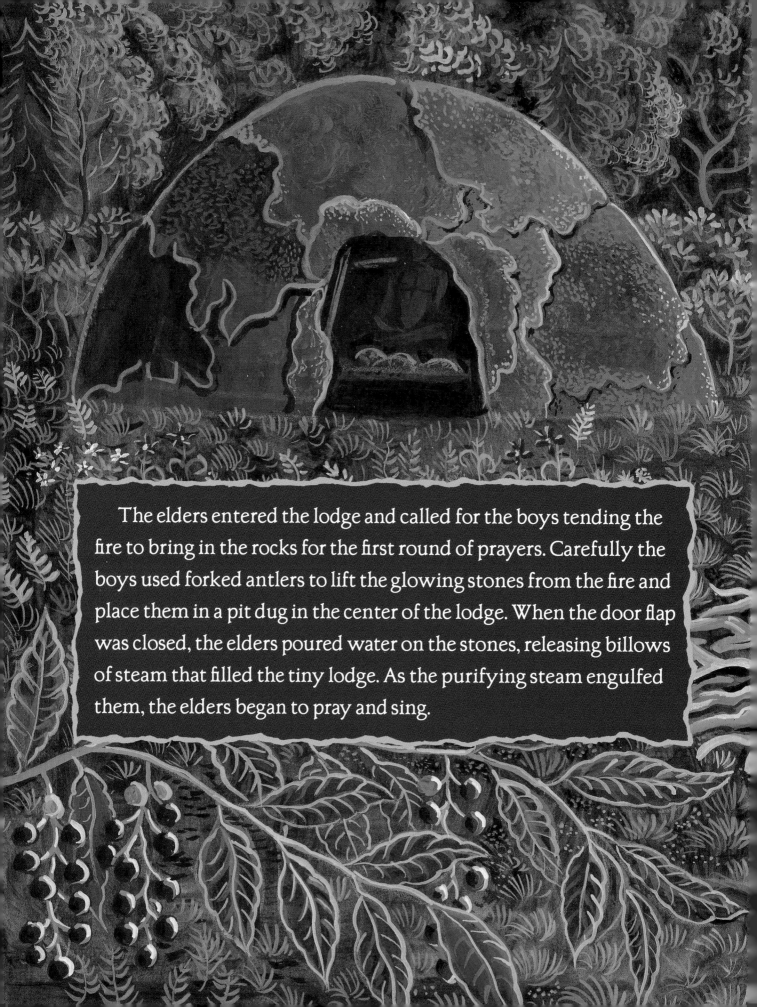

The elders entered the lodge and called for the boys tending the fire to bring in the rocks for the first round of prayers. Carefully the boys used forked antlers to lift the glowing stones from the fire and place them in a pit dug in the center of the lodge. When the door flap was closed, the elders poured water on the stones, releasing billows of steam that filled the tiny lodge. As the purifying steam engulfed them, the elders began to pray and sing.

Three times the wise ones raised the flap and called for more rocks. At the beginning of the fourth round one young boy, preparing to lift a large stone on his forked antler, heard a great POP! as the stone split into two pieces.

"Grandparents," he called, "this last stone has broken."

"They do that sometimes, Grandson," came a voice from the lodge. "It is the heat from the fire." The boy looked down into the glowing heart of the broken stone and slowly an idea began to grow.

When the ceremony was over and the elders had left the lodge,
the boy hurried to speak to them.

"Grandparents, heat can split stones and the Windigo is made of

stone. Could heat destroy the Windigo?" As the elders listened to the boy's words, they began to smile. Perhaps the spirits *had* shown them a way to stay in the land they loved so much.

The next day the young men of the village went into the forest and began to dig. They dug until they had made a great pit in the earth, as deep as the tallest tree was tall. Very carefully the women covered the top of it with branches, earth, leaves, and grass until the great pit was completely hidden.

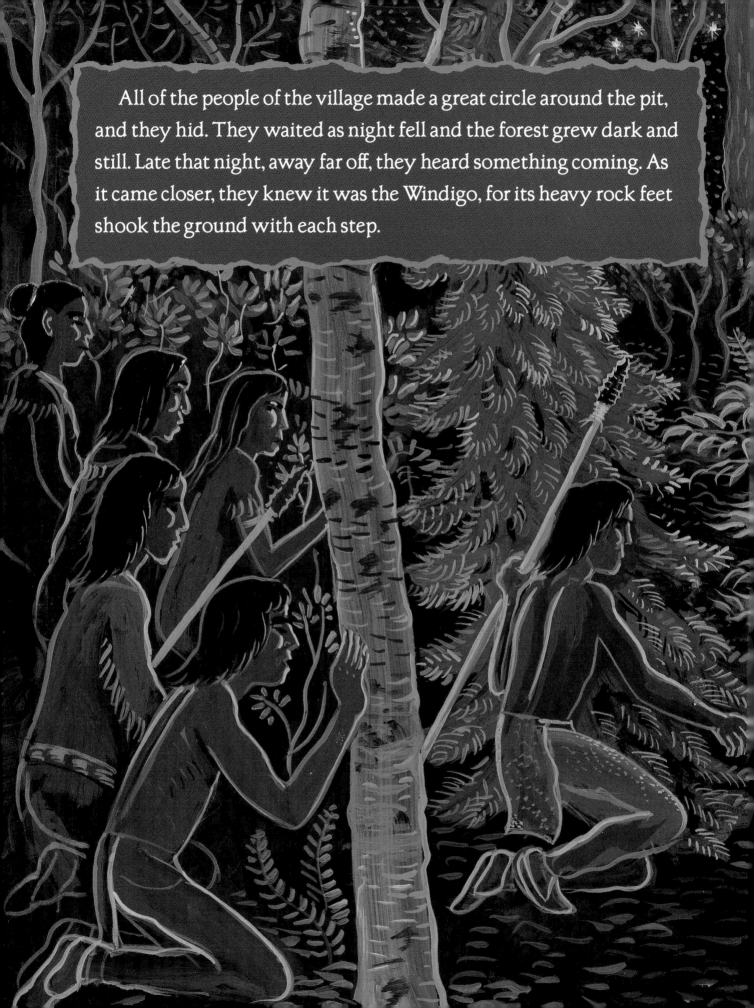

All of the people of the village made a great circle around the pit, and they hid. They waited as night fell and the forest grew dark and still. Late that night, away far off, they heard something coming. As it came closer, they knew it was the Windigo, for its heavy rock feet shook the ground with each step.

The people covered their faces so that no one would look into the eyes of the Windigo as it came closer and closer. Finally the Windigo put one heavy rock foot down on top of that pit and fell through to the bottom with a great CRASH!

Quickly the people rushed from their hiding places and ran to the
pit. Each person carried a log, some branches or brush—anything
that would burn. They piled all the wood down on top of that
Windigo, and then one old woman took a burning coal and tossed
it into the pit!

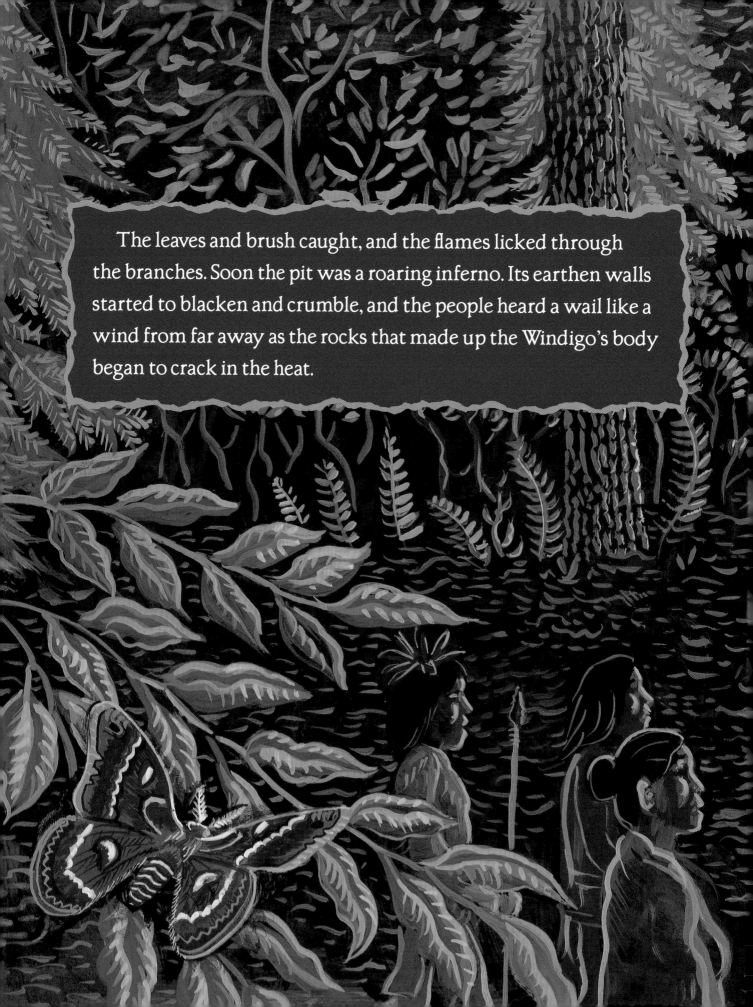

The leaves and brush caught, and the flames licked through the branches. Soon the pit was a roaring inferno. Its earthen walls started to blacken and crumble, and the people heard a wail like a wind from far away as the rocks that made up the Windigo's body began to crack in the heat.

Then everyone heard a terrible scream as the Windigo's heart
exploded in its great stone chest. But inside that scream was a voice —
a tiny little voice, almost like a buzzing sound that each person

heard right next to his ear. It said, "You can burn me up, but you won't be rid of me! The Windigo will haunt this land forever! I'll be eating the people for generations to come!"

As the voice fell silent, the burning piles of logs collapsed, sending billows of smoke and thousands and thousands of ashes floating out into the air. Each tiny ash turned into an insect that swooped and whined and bit the people before it flew away into the forest.

So you can see that the Windigo kept his promise. In the form of mosquitoes, he has been eating the people ever since that day. But now he can only take one bite at a time!

AUTHOR'S NOTE

THERE IS REALLY NO SUCH THING AS A "NATIVE AMERICAN" STORY. The stories, like the people, belong to many tribes, many nations. We are Cherokee. We are Cree. We are Navajo. And so are the tales we tell.

This story, then, requires a bit of explanation. Though it is based on several stories told by tribes in the north, from the Tlingit of Northwest Canada to the Cree of the Eastern Woodlands, this version is essentially my own creation.

Many years ago, I stood next to a roaring campfire with a gathering of storytellers and folk musicians in northern Wisconsin. I had just told a story about a Cree trickster's run-in with a gang of angry hornets. My friend Bruce "Utah" Phillips said that he had heard about a story someplace involving a monster that the people burned, and the ashes turned into the plague we know as mosquitoes. I knew the monster Bruce was talking about had to be the Windigo, having heard many Windigo stories from my adopted brother, Chippewa-Cree storyteller Ron Evans. In a Cree tale about the destruction of the Windigo, the insects created from its ashes are biting blackflies.

Drawing on the memories of those stories, I began to weave this tale. A Tlingit variation called "How Mosquitoes Came to Be," retold from a 19th-century English source, has appeared in *American Indian Myths and Legends*, edited by Richard Erdoes and Alfonso Ortiz, and *Favorite Folktales from Around the World*, edited by Jane Yolen.

A note must also be made about the sweat lodge ceremony depicted in the story. It is painted in broad strokes, with very general descriptions. As with everything else, sweat ceremonies vary from tribe to tribe. The prayers, the songs, the very material from which lodges are constructed, all of these will be different among different nations. For that reason, and because many traditional peoples are very protective of their own rituals, the ceremony depicted here does not represent the specific spiritual tradition of any one tribe. Finally, the character of the young boy at the sweat lodge fire is my own creation, inspired by a real incident in my family.